Written & illustrated by Phillip Reed
(info@phillipreed.net)

This book is dedicated to my Father, Derek Reed,
... still miss you Dad X

THANK YOU...!!

I really appreciate you reading my book and I hope you enjoy it.

If you do, please consider leaving me a review to let other readers know about it.

If you like this story you can read more about Kookie in...
Kookie Koala and The Problem

"With fabulous illustrations, this inviting book shows children the different ways we respond to our problems with a clever story. I totally love the concept and the fun twist at the end." – Sally, primary school teacher

KOOKIE KOALA AND THE Pack of Lies

WRITTEN & ILLUSTRATED BY PHILLIP REED

Kookie was about to
perform a magic trick,
and for a wand he used
Grandad's walking stick.

He wanted to make his
cuddly bunny disappear,
so that he could make his
friends all laugh and cheer.

MAGIC SHOW

He waved his wand around
and gave the table a tap,

but he did it too hard and
the stick went SNAP!

SNAP

Grandad heard the noise and asked,

"what was that sound?"

"Oh, nothing," said Kookie,

as he shamefully frowned.

He told a lie so that he didn't get into trouble,

but didn't know now his problems were about to double.

Because appearing out of
nowhere like a magic trick,

was the word "Lie" and
so he had to think quick.

Lie
MAGIC
SHOW

Kookie was in a bother now,
this was no joke,
so he hastily hid the
lie under his cloak.

He didn't want Grandad
to see what he had done,
he was afraid he might stop
him from having his fun.

"I have to go, Grandad,
it's dinner time."
Is what Kookie said.

As he spoke those words, another lie appeared on his head.

He ran all the way home
hiding this one in his hat,

but he bumped into his friends,
who wanted to chat.

He said. "Er...No magic today, Grandad has hurt his toe."

This made them sad as they wanted to see his show.

But this was not true and
he had told another lie,
and this time the word
seemed to fall from the sky.

It landed on his friend's
head with a loud thump,
Kookie grabbed it quick while
his friend nursed the lump.

THUMP!
Lie
MAGIC SHOW

"What just fell on my head?"
His friend was calling.
"Nothing," Kookie said as he
caught another lie falling.

Lie
Lie
MAGIC SHOW
Lie

When he got home he
was surprised to find,
that one more lie
had followed behind.

Where this one had come
from Kookie did not know,
he had told no more
lies since a while ago.

Lie
Lie
Lie

Kookie could not
believe his eyes,
as now there was
a whole pack of lies.

He was sad and sat with
a face full of gloom,
as he watched the lies
bounce around his room.

Lie
Lie
Lie
Lie
Lie

At bedtime poor Kookie
could not get to sleep,
as all night long, on his
bed, they would leap.

Lie
lie
Lie
Lie
Lie

The next day Grandad
came knocking at his door,
Kookie hid the lies but
out they did pour.

"Ah," Grandad said.
"I see what you're going through.
Tell me what happened
and then I can help you."

Kookie fetched the stick
that he had broken,
and told Grandad all the
lies he had spoken.

Then something happened that they thought was weird.

The word " TRUTH ", in large letters suddenly appeared.

At first the word TRUTH
looked a bit scary,

but Kookie saw that it made
all the lies seem wary,

and just like a sheepdog
it chased the lies away.

Leaving only one lie
that decided to stay.

TRUTH
Lie
Lie
Lie
Lie
Lie

This had been the last
to appear at his door,
and now it just fell
apart on the floor.

"This was the worst one,"
said Grandad with a sigh.
"This one made you think
it was ok to lie."

"You see not all lies
out loud are spoken.
and this lie to yourself,
now lies broken."

"You have learnt that lies can
hurt both you and your friends.

So your show you should
perform to make amends.

You can use the letter 'i'
as a wand in your trick,

and I can use the 'L'
as a new walking stick."

So Kookie performed for
his friends, who did cheer,

by making the last
letter ‘e’ disappear.

MAGIC SHOW
CORN

Now all the lies have gone,
but you must still beware,

by being careful what you
say as they are still out there!

THE END.

Printed in Great Britain
by Amazon

64726502R00024